My "u" Sound Box®

(This book uses only the short "u" sound in the story line. Words beginning
with the long "u" sound are included at the end of the book.)

Library of Congress Cataloging-in-Publication Data
Moncure, Jane Belk.
My "u" sound box / by Jane Belk Moncure; illustrated by Colin King.
p. cm.
Summary: A little girl fills her sound box with many words beginning with the letter "u."
ISBN 1-56766-787-2 (lib. reinforced : alk. paper)
[1. Alphabet.] I. King, Colin, ill. II. Title.
PZ7.M739 Myu   2000
[E]—dc21   99-056566

My "u"
Sound Box®

Jane Belk Moncure

illustrated by Colin King

The Child's World®

Little  had a box.

"I will find things that begin
with my 'u' sound," she said.

"I will put them into my sound  box."

"First, I will find an umbrella."

"I will run, run, run

to find an umbrella."

Why did Little  u get under the box?

Why was the box upside down?

Little  found an umbrella.

She found lots of umbrellas.

She put one umbrella over her head.
Did she put the other umbrellas

into her box?

She did.

Just then, the sun came out.

Little u put the umbrella down.

But then the rain came down again.

Little u put the umbrella up.

Then she saw some underclothes.

They were getting wet.

She took the underclothes off the line.

She put them into her box.

Little  took the underclothes upstairs.

She put the underclothes away.

"Now," she said, "I can play
under my umbrella."

She went out in the rain.

"I can run through a

puddle,"

she said. "What fun!"

Then Little found an ugly duckling.

The ugly duckling was grumpy.

She put the ugly duckling into her box.

"Do not be grumpy," she said.
"You will grow up to be beautiful."

Just then, her uncle came by.

He was getting wet, so

Little gave her uncle

an umbrella.

Next, an umpire came by.

"Can you help us?" he said.

"We are playing baseball in the rain.

We need umbrellas."

Little  u said, "I have a box full of umbrellas."

She gave the umpire an umbrella.

Then she gave everyone an umbrella.

underclothes

ugly
duckling

umbrella

umpire

uncle

What fun they had in the rain.

Can you read these words

with Little  ?

undershirt

Uncle Sam

usher

umbrella bird

umbrella tree

Little 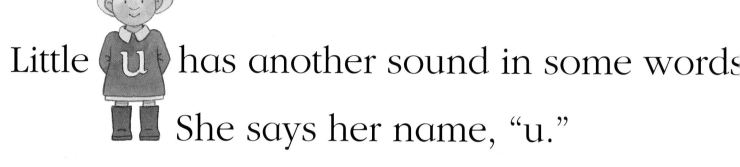 u has another sound in some words.

She says her name, "u."

Can you read these words?

Listen for Little u 's name.

ukulele

uniform

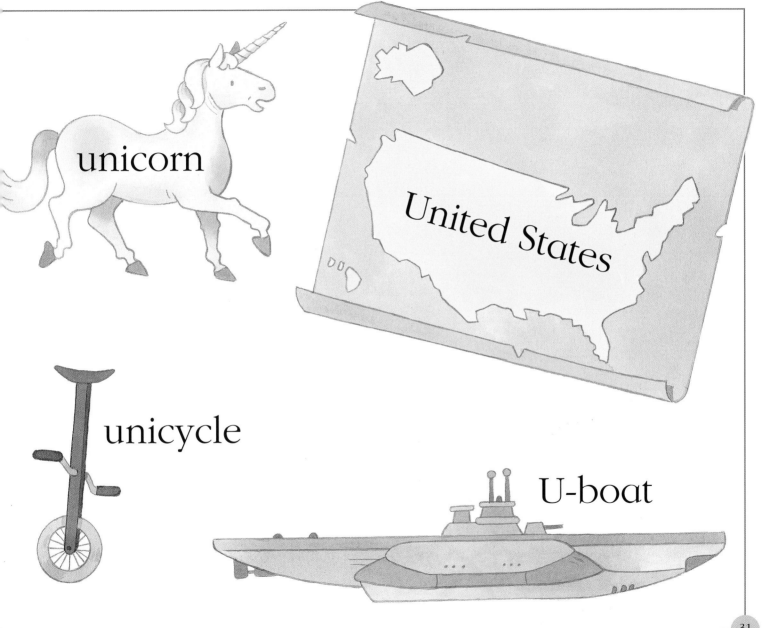

unicorn

United States

unicycle

U-boat

ABOUT THE AUTHOR AND ILLUSTRATOR

Jane Belk Moncure began her writing career when she was in kindergarten. She has never stopped writing. Many of her children's stories and poems have been published, to the delight of young readers, including her son Jim, whose childhood experiences found their way into many of her books.

Mrs. Moncure's writing is based upon an active career in early childhood education. A recipient of an M.A. degree from Columbia University, Mrs. Moncure has taught and directed nursery, kindergarten, and primary grade programs in California, New York, Virginia, and North Carolina. As a former member of the faculties of Virginia Commonwealth University and the University of Richmond, she taught prospective teachers in early childhood education.

Mrs. Moncure has travelled extensively abroad, studying early childhood programs in the United Kingdom, The Netherlands, and Switzerland. She was the first president of the Virginia Association for Early Childhood Education and received its award for outstanding service to young children.

A resident of North Carolina, Mrs. Moncure is currently a full-time writer and educational consultant. She is married to Dr. James A. Moncure, former vice president of Elon College.

Colin King studied at the Royal College of Art, London. He started his freelance career as an illustrator, working for magazines and advertising agencies.

He began drawing pictures for children's books in 1976 and has illustrated over sixty titles to date.

Included in a wide variety of subjects are a best-selling children's encyclopedia and books about spies and detectives.

His books have been translated into several languages, including Japanese and Hebrew. He has four grown-up children and lives in Suffolk, England, with his wife, three dogs, and a cat.